Pick a Powerpuff Path

Bubbles and the Opposite Potion

by Catherine Hapka

Scholastic Inc.
New York • Toronto • London • Auckland • Sydney
Mexico City • New Delhi • Hong Kong • Buenos Aires

ISBN 0-439-33252-4

Cover and interior illustrations by Christopher Cook

Inked by John and Philip Hom

Designed by Mark Neston

12 11 10 9 8 7 6 5 4 3 2 1 2 3 4 5 6 7/0

Printed in the U. S. A.

First Scholastic printing, April 2002

Read This First!

Sugar…Spice…and Everything Nice…

These were the ingredients chosen to create the perfect little girl. But Professor Utonium accidentally added an extra ingredient to the concoction—Chemical X!

And thus, The Powerpuff Girls were born! Using their ultra superpowers, Blossom, Bubbles, and Buttercup have dedicated their lives to fighting crime and the forces of evil!

But the Professor didn't stop with creating The Powerpuff Girls. His latest creation is the opposite potion—but when the crazy concoction gets spread all over Townsville and everyone starts acting the opposite of their usual selves, things get topsy-turvy. And The Powerpuff Girls are the only ones who can put things right!

In each Pick a Powerpuff Path, you will take on the role of one of the characters and help save the day. In this adventure, you will be Bubbles, the sweet, mild-mannered, animal-loving Powerpuff Girl…. Or is she? Now that Bubbles and her sisters have been "oppositized," almost anything can happen!

The story will change depending on the choices you make. Follow the directions to see how your story turns out. When you're done, you can start over, make new choices, and read a completely different story.

So what are you waiting for? Slow down…or is it, hurry up, and start reading!

The city of Townsville! Home of the cutest—and most powerful—superheroes around, The Powerpuff Girls, and their creator, scientific genius Professor Utonium. What's that you're mixing up in your lab right now, Professor?

"Watch, Girls," the Professor said, holding up a beaker of purple liquid. "My opposite potion is ready to test. I'm going to try to turn a butterfly back into a caterpillar."

Bubbles wrinkled her nose. "Why, Professor?" she asked. "Butterflies are pretty. Caterpillars are just icky bugs." Bubbles loved animals that were pretty, cute, or fuzzy, but she couldn't bring herself to like bugs.

"It's my entry in the Townsville Science Expo Contest to find the most interesting scientific concoction using ordinary household ingredients," the Professor explained.

Brrinngg! The Powerpuff Girls' hotline phone was ringing. Blossom picked it up and listened.

"The Third Bank of Townsville is being robbed!" Blossom cried. "We'd better hurry!"

As The Powerpuff Girls raced for the door, they bumped into the Professor. The potion flew out of his hand, splashing purple liquid everywhere.

"Oops!" Bubbles said. "Sorry, Professor!"

There was no time to stick around and help mop up. The Girls zoomed off toward the bank. As they flew, they left trails of pink, blue, and green. Mixed with the other colors were squiggles of, you guessed it, purple.

"Ick," Blossom complained. "I got purple goo all over me."

"Me, too." Buttercup shook some of the Professor's potion off her arm.

The potion drifted in the wind, floating down all over Townsville as the Girls swooped toward the bank.

Bubbles gasped. Something was sitting on the sidewalk. Something terrifyingly furry and small.

A puppy!

"Girls!" Bubbles cried, pointing at the puppy. "Look out!"

"Bubbles, what's wrong?" Blossom asked. "It's not like you to be petrified of a puppy. That's strange...."

Bubbles kept a careful eye on the puppy while she waited for her super-smart sister to explain why she, Bubbles, would be scared of a cute puppy. But Blossom just looked more and more confused.

Meanwhile, Buttercup glanced nervously into the bank. "Those robbers look awfully tough," she whispered. "Maybe we should just go home."

"Strange," Blossom repeated blankly. "Um, wait. What was I talking about?"

Suddenly, Bubbles realized what was happening. "The Professor's potion!" she cried. "A caterpillar is the *opposite* of a butterfly. We're all acting the opposite of our usual selves! Blossom, you're usually quick and clever—now you can't figure out a simple problem. Buttercup, you're normally brave and bold—now you're a wimp. I usually love all sorts of cute creatures, and now...."

Blossom still looked confused, and Buttercup was so nervous she was shaking. Bubbles could see that it was up to her now to be the leader. Luckily, she was feeling much more daring and confident than usual.

What should she do first?

If Bubbles leads her sisters into the bank to take care of the robbers first, turn to page 48.

If the Girls head home so the Professor can fix the opposite problem first, turn to page 14.

"Princess might remember who has her pearl," Bubbles said. "That's probably the easiest way to find one."

Moments later, the Girls had retrieved Princess from her mountaintop retreat and set her down near the park.

"Okay, Princess," Bubbles said. "Think. Who has that black pearl?"

Princess scratched her chin. "Hmm. It's hard to remember. I gave away lots of stuff today."

"Think harder," Bubbles urged. "You *must* remember who took the pearl."

"Was it that nice Mojo Jojo?" Princess mused. "No, I gave him a ruby pin for his cape. I know I gave something to the Mayor.... Wait, that was my emerald tiara...."

Maybe Princess wasn't going to be able to help after all. . . .

"Aha!" Princess cried. "I remember. I gave my black pearl to that furry fellow who talks funny. You know—Fuzzy Lumpkins!"

"Uh-oh," Buttercup whispered. "Fuzzy will never give us that pearl!"

Normally, Buttercup would be right. Fuzzy was greedy and grasping, surly and selfish. But maybe he had been oppositized, too!

"Let's go to his cabin," Bubbles said.

The Girls flew to the woods outside of Townsville. Fuzzy Lumpkins greeted them on the porch. "Please come in!" he cried. "Would you like some tea? Perhaps a slice of homemade pie? Or would you care to pluck out a tune on old Joe?" He pointed to his beloved banjo.

"No, thanks." Bubbles was happy to see Fuzzy acting the opposite of his usual self. "But we *could* use a black pearl if you happen to have one."

"Of course!" Fuzzy immediately held out the black pearl. "Anything I have is yours."

The Girls thanked him and rushed back to Townsville. The Professor added the pearl to his potion.

"It's finished!" he said, holding out the container of bubbling purple liquid. "Now all you have to do is spread it over Townsville."

Continue on page 64.

Bubbles decided that the most important thing to do now was to check in with the Mayor, so the Girls flew to his office. The Mayor looked up from his desk, where he was busily scribbling on a notepad.

"Greetings, Girls," he said. "How splendid to see you!"

Bubbles explained about the opposite potion and its effect on the people of Townsville, although she didn't expect the Mayor to be that helpful.

But the Mayor listened carefully, and when Bubbles was done, he said, "Ah, I see. A stray scientific formula is causing the citizens of our fair city to transform into the opposites of their usual selves, and we need an antidote."

"Are you feeling okay, Mayor?" Bubbles asked. It wasn't like the Mayor to figure things out so fast—or use such big words. His personality was strong, but his brain was weak.

"Undoubtedly!" the Mayor replied. "I'm not sure about poor Ms. Bellum, though."

The Girls looked at the Mayor's assistant. The usually brilliant Ms. Bellum was bent over a table fiddling with a steaming teapot.

"Oh, phooey," she exclaimed. "I can't remember. Am I supposed to pour the tea onto your desk or out the window?"

She scratched her head.

"Neither for now, my good woman," the Mayor replied. "We must concoct an antidote. All I need are a few common household items...."

Ms. Bellum snapped her fingers. "Wait!" she cried. "That reminds me. I know *exactly* what we should do now."

Bubbles wasn't sure what to do. Normally she would listen to Ms. Bellum's plan. She had more sense in her pinky finger than the Mayor had in his whole head.

But today *wasn't* normal. Maybe it would be better to listen to the Mayor.

If Bubbles decides to follow her usual instincts and listens to Ms. Bellum, turn to page 32.

If Bubbles decides to listen to the Mayor's plan instead, turn to page 28.

"We've got to stop them!" Bubbles cried. "Who knows how much more trouble the Amoeba Boys might cause?"

The Powerpuff Girls took off after the criminals. It wasn't easy to follow them. The Amoeba Boys kept cleverly leaving false trails and tricking the Girls.

But, finally, the Girls caught up with the Amoeba Boys near the Third Bank of Townsville. "We've got you now, Amoeba Boys!" Bubbles shouted.

She grabbed Bossman. Blossom managed to tackle Slim. Buttercup nervously headed toward Tiny. The Amoeba Boys might be smart now, but they were still no match for The Powerpuff Girls' superpowers!

The Girls couldn't put the Amoeba Boys in jail, though—the single-celled criminals would have slipped through the bars. So the Girls locked the Amoeba Boys up in a bank vault.

"There! We're finished!" Blossom cried happily. "Let's go home and play!"

"We can't," Bubbles reminded her sister, who usually refused to play until all of her work—and crime-fighting—were done. "We still have to find that antidote!"

"But how?" Buttercup asked fearfully.

"We've got to find the Professor," Bubbles said. Realizing what time it was, she added, "Maybe he's having lunch. We should check all his favorite hangouts."

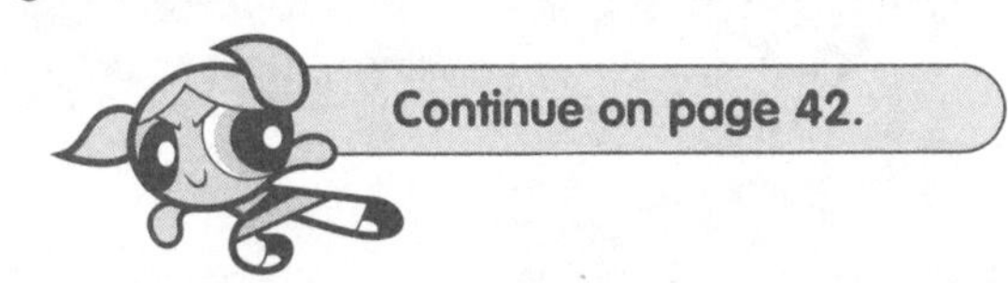
Continue on page 42.

As Bubbles turned away, Princess grabbed Bubbles's arm.

"Wait," she cried. "I didn't give you guys anything!" She dug through her pile of things until she found three matching diamond bracelets. "Here! They're perfect for you!"

"Um, thanks," Bubbles muttered.

But Princess wasn't finished. "Will you please, please do me a favor?" she begged. "Will you carry me to the top of Townsville Mountain? There's a cave there that would be perfect for my new simple life. But there's no way to get there except by flying."

Bubbles paused to think. On the one hand, she and her sisters were awfully busy trying to save Townsville. On the other hand, this could be their chance to get Princess out of Townsville and stop all of her villainous schemes forever!

If Bubbles tells Princess they're too busy to help her, turn to 45.

If Bubbles decides to give Princess exactly what she's asking for, turn to page 58.

"Let's go home, Girls," Bubbles said. "We've got to get Townsville back to normal before things get even weirder."

As the Girls zoomed over the city, Bubbles looked down, wondering what other strange problems the opposite potion was causing. She noticed a familiar figure lurking in an alley.

"Uh-oh," she cried, skidding to a stop in midair. "That's Mojo Jojo!"

Buttercup gasped with fear. "Oh, no!"

"Who's Mojo Jojo?" Blossom asked.

"Mojo Jojo is the most dangerous criminal in Townsville, remember?" Bubbles explained patiently to her opposite potion-muddled sister. "He used to be the Professor's lab monkey, but he turned evil and became our greatest enemy. If he's causing trouble, it can't wait."

Bubbles sped toward the caped monkey. "Mojo Jojo, stop right there!" she yelled.

Mojo looked up. "Ah, how wonderful! It's my favorite adorable superheroes, The Powerpuff Girls!" he cried, his face stretching into a huge grin. "I am so overjoyed, I fear I might burst. Yes, I may explode with happiness at being in the presence of such charming and delightful Girls! My joy at seeing you three sweet crime fighters is so great that I can hardly contain myself!"

Blossom looked confused. "Hey, Bubbles," she said. "I thought you said he was our greatest enemy."

"I guess Mojo has been oppositized, too," Bubbles replied.

Or had he?

Bubbles narrowed her eyes suspiciously. Mojo was very clever, and he was always looking for new ways to trick The Powerpuff Girls. What if this was one of his plots? What if he was just *pretending* to be oppositized?

Bubbles needed to figure it out, but Mojo was distracting her by praising The Powerpuff Girls even more. "Go away for a minute, Mojo," Bubbles told him.

"Right away," he agreed. "I shall depart immediately. Mojo Jojo will vacate the area as The Powerpuff Girls request. Here I am, leaving right now, as you wish."

Mojo hurried away. Bubbles sighed with relief. Now she could think about what to do next.

If Bubbles decides to chase after Mojo and drag him off to jail (to make sure that he doesn't commit any crimes), turn to page 62.

If Bubbles decides to forget about Mojo and continue on to find the Professor, turn to page 22.

Bubbles flew off in search of her sisters. Were they at the park patrolling for problems? At the Third Bank of Townsville watching for robbers? In the streets checking for citizens in need? Bubbles checked all of those places and more, but there was no sign of her sisters anywhere.

Then she realized her mistake. Blossom and Buttercup were acting the *opposite* of their usual selves. Where was the *last* place they would go at a time like this?

Finally, Bubbles figured out where they must be. Moments later, she had flown to their home.

"Hello?" she shouted. "Anybody home?"

Bubbles floated into the bedroom she shared with her sisters.

"Hello?" she called again. "Blossom? Buttercup?"

"Bubbles?" a nervous voice squeaked. "Is that you?"

Bubbles peered under the bed. Her sisters were huddled there together. Buttercup still looked terrified. Blossom just looked befuddled.

Bubbles dragged her sisters out. "Come on," she urged. "We have to find an antidote to the opposite potion—pronto!"

The Girls searched the whole house. But there was no sign of the scientist. Now what? Blossom had no idea, and Buttercup was too scared to think straight.

Maybe the Professor was eating lunch at his favorite restaurant, and Bubbles would find him there. Or maybe it would be better to give up looking for the Professor and go where Bubbles *knew* there would be scientists—the Townsville Science Expo Center!

If Bubbles decides to go to the Professor's favorite restaurant, turn to page 42.

If Bubbles decides to go to the Townsville Science Expo Center, turn to page 31.

Oppositized or not, Bubbles wasn't going to trust the robbers to go to jail by themselves!

"Sorry," she said. "I think we'd better come along just in case."

So The Powerpuff Girls collared the cooperative criminals and flew them to the city jail. Soon, the robbers were locked in a cell.

"That takes care of that," Bubbles announced. She looked around at the jailers. "You guys had better keep a close eye on these...."

Her voice drifted off. Was it her imagination, or were the jailers looking kind of sneaky?

"Grab 'em, guys!" one of the jailers shouted suddenly. "Let's lock up those rotten Powerpuff Girls once and for all!"

The jailers rushed toward The Powerpuff Girls. "Eek!" Buttercup squealed, flying through the window at full speed.

"Wait for me!" Blossom called worriedly. "I don't know the way home!"

Before Bubbles could stop her, Blossom flew off after Buttercup.

"Oh, no!" Bubbles moaned. Now she was left all alone!

By herself, Bubbles quickly overpowered the jailers and locked them in an empty cell. But she still had a big problem—she had no idea where her sisters had gone.

Now what should she do?

If Bubbles decides to find her sisters, turn to page 16.

If Bubbles decides to head home alone, figuring the sooner she finds an antidote to the opposite potion, the better, turn to page 52.

"It's more important to see how far this stuff has spread," Bubbles decided. "We'll just have to trust those oppositized robbers to go to jail by themselves."

She led the way out of the bank. Luckily, the scary puppy was gone, but there were lots of other strange things happening outside.

A baby was pushing its mother through the park in a stroller. A delivery man was rushing from house to house grabbing back all the packages he'd just delivered. A window washer was leaving dirty handprints on every clean window in sight.

"Wow," Bubbles said as The Powerpuff Girls flew over Townsville. "The opposite potion is all over town. It must have floated everywhere when we flew over the city."

"Uh-oh," Buttercup said, her voice trembling. "I think I see the Gangreen Gang. We should get out of here."

"Are you kidding? We're not scared of those punks." Bubbles stared at the gang of green-skinned goons. They were bending over some small children. "They're probably up to no good, as usual," she muttered.

Then she paused. Nobody was acting the way they usually did. Was the Gangreen Gang any different? Maybe they should wait and see what the Gang was up to. Then again, they didn't have any time to waste. Perhaps they should go ahead and confront them, just to be on the safe side.

If Bubbles and her sisters observe the Gangreen Gang first to see what they're up to, turn to page 30.

If Bubbles and her sisters confront the Gangreen Gang immediately, turn to page 25.

"We need to talk to the Professor!" Bubbles said. "Now!"

The Girls sped toward home.

"Professor?" Bubbles called as they flew into their house. "Where are you?"

"Hello?" a familiar voice replied. "Who's there?"

It was the Professor. But why didn't he recognize Bubbles's voice? Maybe because he was too involved in concocting an antidote to the opposite potion? Bubbles hoped that was the reason!

But when Bubbles and her sisters flew into the living room, the Professor was slumped on the couch staring at the TV. The news was showing the strange things going on in Townsville.

The Professor blinked. "Hello, little girls," he said vaguely. "You look sort of familiar. Are you here to sell candy?"

"Oh, no!" Bubbles cried. "The Professor has been oppositized, too!"

Buttercup flew around the room. Usually, she was very good at flying. But the potion had made her clumsy as well as frightened. She bumped into the table next to the couch. There was a beaker of purple liquid sitting on the table. It started to topple.

"Uh-oh," Bubbles cried. "That looks like more opposite potion!"

She leaped forward, trying to catch the beaker—too late! It splashed onto the Professor.

"Oh, dear." The Professor blinked at the TV. "My potion is affecting all of Townsville! We must do something!"

"Professor!" Bubbles exclaimed. "You're smart again!"

The Professor smiled. "Yes, thanks to Buttercup's little accident." He led the way to his lab and grabbed another container of purple potion.

"But, Professor," Bubbles said, "that looks like the same potion that made you dumb in the first place."

"Right," the Professor said. "You see, releasing the potion once made everything go opposite. Releasing it again will reverse everything."

"I don't get it," Blossom said blankly.

"I do!" Bubbles cried. "The opposite of opposite is the same!"

"Right again," the Professor said. "Now hold still, Girls...."

He sprinkled a little purple potion on them.

"That should put things back to normal for you three," he said. "Now you'd better do the same for the rest of Townsville."

"Right away, Professor!" all three Girls cried at once.

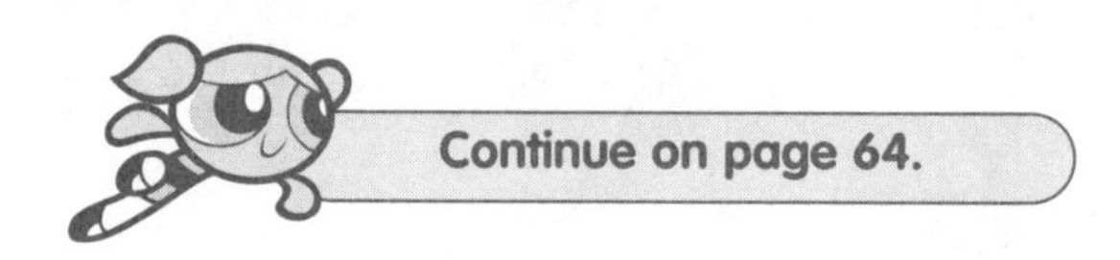

Bubbles decided to block off the part of the road where the Pokey Oaks kids were playing. She knocked over a few trees to keep the cars out of those lanes.

"That will have to do for now," she told herself. "Now, I need to get home and find the Professor! The sooner we have an antidote, the better."

Bubbles flew as fast as she could. But when she got home, the Professor was nowhere to be found.

Oh, no! Bubbles thought. *Where could he be?*

She stopped to think. Maybe he'd gone to the Townsville Science Expo Center to ask the other scientists for help in concocting an antidote. But it was also possible that he could be almost anywhere else in Townsville. Maybe it would be better to find her sisters first so they could all search together.

If Bubbles decides to head to the Townsville Science Expo Center to look for the Professor, turn to page 50.

If Bubbles decides to look for her sisters first, turn to page 46.

"Those troublemakers are always up to no good," Bubbles decided. "Come on, Girls. Let's get 'em!"

Bubbles flew down and grabbed the nearest Gangreen, Snake.

"Hey, Bubblessss!" he cried. "Ssssstop! You're hurting me!"

Snake started crying. Bubbles stopped, perplexed.

"What's the matter with you?" she demanded.

"Please, Powerpuff Girls!" Little Arturo exclaimed. "Don't hurt us. We were just helping those nice little kids across the street. At least we *thought* they were nice—until they started kicking us in the shins."

Bubbles realized that she had made a mistake in attacking the Gangreen Gang—the Gangreen Gang had been oppositized, too, and now they were good and helpful, instead of being nasty punks!

"Sorry about that," Bubbles said sheepishly. She looked at her sisters. "That potion is even more powerful than I thought. We need expert help fast!"

But who could help them the quickest? They could fly home and see if the Professor had an answer. But the Townsville Science Expo Center was just down the street. Maybe they should check there first to see if one of the geniuses could help.

If the Girls race home to the Professor immediately, turn to page 22.

If the Girls rush to the Townsville Science Expo Center first, turn to page 31.

Bubbles started dragging kids to safety. It wasn't easy. Elmer Sglue spat at her when she picked him up. Mary tried to bite her. The Floijoidson twins called her names.

Finally, all the Pokey Oaks kids were standing safely at the side of the road.

"I'm bored," Lloyd Floijoidson announced. "Come on, Floyd. Let's go play in the road some more!"

"No!" Bubbles shouted. "Will you stay here if I give you some candy?"

"Candy? *Blech!*" Elmer made a face. "We *hate* candy."

"Not me!" Ms. Keane announced, looking up from her comic book. "I love it!" She wiped her chocolate-smeared mouth on her sleeve.

"Right," Bubbles muttered. "I keep forgetting, we Girls oppositized everybody."

Bubbles noticed a grocery store across the highway. Zipping over, she grabbed some items off the shelves. When she went to pay, the shopkeeper waved her off.

"No, no," he insisted. "I don't want your money. Take anything you want!"

Bubbles didn't have time to argue with the shopkeeper, who would ordinarily have insisted that he be paid. "Okay, thanks!"

Bubbles flew back to the class and handed Ms. Keane a gooey, sticky candy bar. Then she pulled out the other items she'd gotten from the store.

"Look, everyone!" she shouted. "Lima beans and Brussels sprouts!"

"Hooray!" the kids cheered. They rushed over and started gobbling down the vegetables.

Just then, Bubbles heard someone shouting her name. She turned and saw the Professor racing toward her. Blossom and Buttercup were right behind him.

"Professor?" Bubbles said, wondering if he'd been oppositized, too. "Are you—um—okay?"

"Don't worry." The Professor smiled. "When the opposite potion got me, I forgot everything I knew. But then I stepped in the puddle where the beaker spilled, and everything came back to me! That's the antidote!" He held up a jar of purple potion. "The opposite of opposite is the same. All you Girls have to do is spread the potion over Townsville again, and everything will go back to normal."

That sounded great to Bubbles. "Let's go, Girls!" she cried, grabbing the potion.

Continue on page 64.

Bubbles realized that on such a topsy-turvy day, it made sense to do the opposite of what she would usually do. So, she decided to listen to the Mayor.

"Okay, Mayor," she said. "What's your plan?"

"Come with me." The Mayor hurried out of his office.

The Powerpuff Girls and Ms. Bellum followed the Mayor to the drugstore across the street. The Mayor started grabbing things off the shelves.

"What are you doing, Mayor?" Blossom asked.

"These are the ingredients for the antidote, my dear," the Mayor explained. "I've been thinking about it, and it's really quite simple. Now, all I need is a container...."

Bubbles found an empty jar on the shelf. The Mayor started pouring ingredients into it. Soon, he held up a container full of bubbling purple liquid. It looked just like the Professor's potion!

"Problem solved," the Mayor announced. "All you Girls have to do is release this over the city, and all will be back to normal."

Bubbles still wasn't too sure she should be trusting the Mayor to save the day. But what choice did they have?

"All right," she said. "I guess—I *hope*—it can't hurt to try."

She and her sisters grabbed the Mayor's potion and flew out of the store. The Mayor followed them outside.

"Try to scatter the potion as widely and thoroughly as you can," the Mayor suggested. "We want it to take effect across the entire metropolis, you know."

"Yeah," Ms. Bellum added. "And don't hold the jar upside down. I did that with the teapot, and it made a big boo-boo on the rug."

Ms. Bellum's silly comment helped Bubbles make up her mind to try the Mayor's antidote—she had to try to get things back to normal! Bubbles held up the container of purple potion.

"Let's go, Girls!" she exclaimed.

Continue on page 64.

"Let's wait a second and see what the Gangreen Gang is up to," Bubbles decided.

The Powerpuff Girls watched as each member of the Gangreen Gang took a little kid by the hand. They stepped forward carefully, heading for the crosswalk.

"Those bullies aren't harassing little kids this time!" Bubbles cried. "They're helping them to cross the street!"

"They're trying to, anyway," Buttercup added. "Those sweet little kids have turned mean—they keep kicking the Gangreen Gang in the shins!"

Ace, the leader of the Gangreen Gang, turned around.

"Bubbles!" he said happily. "Blossom! Buttercup! We're so happy to see you!"

"You are?" Buttercup asked nervously.

"Of courssssse!" Snake hissed. "We're alwayssss happy to sssssee you Girlsssss. Isss there anything we can do to help you?"

Bubbles exchanged an amazed glance with her sisters. They could certainly use some help. And the Gangreen Gang members were definitely the opposite of their usual unfriendly selves. But even a helpful Gangreen meant trouble...didn't it?

If Bubbles and her sisters decide to accept the Gang's offer of help, turn to page 34.

If Bubbles and her sisters refuse the Gang's offer of help and continue on their own, turn to 35.

"Come on," Bubbles said. "The quicker we get an antidote, the better. And the Townsville Science Expo Center is the closest place we might find it—the scientists there are sure to help us."

She led the way to the center. As soon as the Girls entered, Bubbles spotted a couple of scientists playing tug-of-war with a white lab coat. Another scientist was building a house out of blocks. Yet another was wandering through the halls singing nursery rhymes—and getting the words all wrong!

"Of course!" Bubbles smacked herself on the forehead. "The scientists are oppositized, too. Instead of being brilliant geniuses, they're all imbeciles!"

"What's an imbecile?" Blossom asked.

"Never mind," Bubbles said. "We've got to figure out what to do."

"Waaah!" Buttercup wailed. "I'm scared! I want the Professor!"

It was definitely unlike Buttercup to get so upset, but Bubbles thought that Buttercup actually had the right idea—they needed the Professor! *But where should we look first?* Bubbles wondered.

Continue on page 42.

Ms. Bellum always knew what to do. Maybe the fact that she'd been oppositized wouldn't make any difference.

"Okay, Ms. Bellum," Bubbles said. "What do you have in mind?"

"Come with me," Ms. Bellum replied, leading the way out of the building.

The Mayor followed. "But Girls!" he cried. "I'm quite confident that my plan is foolproof."

"Mine is better," Ms. Bellum insisted. "First, we go in here." She led the Mayor and the Girls into an ice-cream parlor.

"What do we do next?" Buttercup asked.

Ms. Bellum clapped her hands. "Order ice cream, of course!" she cried happily.

Bubbles sighed. *Why* had she decided to listen to Ms. Bellum? The woman was obviously the opposite of her usual, sensible self.

Suddenly, Bubbles noticed that Buttercup was shaking with fear.

"L—look!" Buttercup said. "The Amoeba Boys!"

Bubbles glanced at the single-celled criminals. The troublemaking trio was huddled in a corner of the ice-cream parlor.

"I bet they've been oppositized, too," Bubbles said. "They're probably good now instead of bad."

Most likely, it would only waste more time if they stopped to see what the Amoeba Boys were up to. Or would it?

If Bubbles ignores the Amoeba Boys and decides she and her sisters should leave the ice-cream parlor, turn to page 38.

If Bubbles goes over to see what the Amoeba Boys are talking about, turn to page 40.

"I guess we need all the help we can get," Bubbles said.

She told the Gangreen Gang to find the Professor and tell him what was happening.

"You got it, Bubbles," Little Arturo said eagerly. "You're the boss!"

As the Gang hurried off, Blossom shrugged. "If they're getting the antidote, what are we supposed to be doing?" she asked.

"We're going to keep things from getting too crazy around Townsville," Bubbles replied. "We'd better go check in with the Mayor. Meanwhile, start watching for anything else that looks like trouble."

Buttercup pointed one trembling finger down the street. "Y—you mean like her?"

Bubbles looked where her sister was pointing. "Princess Morbucks!" she cried. The spoiled rich girl was always causing problems for The Powerpuff Girls. "What's *she* doing here?"

If Bubbles leads the way to check on what Princess is up to, turn to page 54.

If the Girls ignore Princess and go to check in with the Mayor, turn to page 10.

"I don't think so, guys," Bubbles said. "Thanks anyway."

Even though the Gangreen Gang *were* acting nice, Bubbles still didn't trust them.

"Are you sure?" Ace said.

Before Bubbles could answer, a shout came from nearby. Bubbles saw a Girl Scout troop racing toward them.

"Look at those jerks!" yelled the troop's khaki-clad leader. "Let's get them!"

The entire Girl Scout troop started attacking the Gangreen Gang.

"Ow!" Big Billy complained as a tiny girl with glasses started pounding on his kneecaps.

"Sssstop that, you bulliessss!" Snake cried as another scout yanked at his hair.

Bubbles frowned. She didn't mind seeing the Gangreen Gang get pounded. But it reminded her just how topsy-turvy Townsville had become, thanks to the opposite potion.

Continue on page 22.

Bubbles decided that Buttercup was right. They could use any grown-up help they could get.

"Okay, let's find help," Bubbles said. "But who should we ask?"

Buttercup immediately stopped crying. "That furry guy over there looks nice, even though I think we've fought him a few times."

Bubbles looked where her sister was pointing. "Fuzzy Lumpkins? You've got to be kidding!" she exclaimed. "What's he doing in Townsville?"

Fuzzy was a rude, selfish, thick-witted hillbilly who lived in a cabin in the woods. He only came to Townsville to cause trouble.

Buttercup shrugged. "It sounds like he's reading from the encyclopedia."

Bubbles realized Buttercup was right. Fuzzy was gesturing with one hand while he held a thick book with the other. He was reading out loud in a dramatic voice.

"I guess that means he's been oppositized, too," Bubbles mused. "And since he's usually the *last* person we would ask for help, maybe that means he should be the *first* one we ask now."

When Fuzzy heard what the Girls needed, he smiled. "I live only to serve others," he said. "Just let me experiment a bit, and I'm sure I can come up with a potion that will help the good people of Townsville."

The Girls waited while Fuzzy hurried into a nearby shop to search for ingredients. Soon, he had mixed up a bubbling purple concoction. It looked exactly like the Professor's original potion!

"Is that the antidote?" Bubbles asked.

"Undoubtedly!" Fuzzy replied.

"Huh?" Blossom said.

"Thanks, Fuzzy!" Bubbles said, taking the container of potion.

Fuzzy waved Bubbles off. "Knowing that I've done something for others is thanks enough for me."

Continue on page 64.

Bubbles figured that the Amoeba Boys were probably even more harmless than usual. She led her sisters out of the ice-cream parlor. The Mayor and Ms. Bellum hurried after them.

"*Now* would you like to hear my plan?" the Mayor asked. "It's quite ingenious, if I do say so myself."

Just then, there was a loud *beep beep* from somewhere nearby.

"The jewelry store!" Buttercup cried, pointing to a shop across the street. "What's going on?"

The shop's door flew open. Bubbles stared in utter surprise as a huge, blob-shaped robot rolled out, still beeping loudly. Its blobby metal arms were full of jewels!

"That robot is robbing the store!" Buttercup cried.

"But who—?" Bubbles began.

Hearing sly laughter behind her, she turned to see the Amoeba Boys rushing out of the ice-cream parlor. They raced past the Girls and hopped into a compartment in the robot's body. A second later, all three of the single-celled criminals, the robot, and all the jewels disappeared in a puff of smoke.

Bubbles realized what must have happened.

"Oh, no!" she exclaimed. "The Amoeba Boys are oppositized, but not the way I thought. I thought they'd become good. Instead, they've changed from being stupid, bumbling villains into brilliant criminal masterminds!"

If the Girls decide to go after the Amoeba Boys, turn to page 12.

If the Girls race home so that the Professor can reverse the potion before the Boys cause more trouble, turn to page 47.

Bubbles sneaked over and hid near the Amoeba Boys' table. They didn't notice her listening.

"...and then we release our army of specially programmed robots," Slim said eagerly. "We'll be able to take over Townsville!"

"Let's go over the plan one more time," Bossman said. "Here's what we do...."

Bossman described the entire plan. Bubbles gasped. It was brilliant! How had such simpleminded criminals come up with a plan to take over Townsville?

And then, she knew. *It's the opposite potion again!* she thought. *It's turned the Amoeba Boys from bumbling fools into criminal masterminds!*

Suddenly, Bubbles had a brilliant idea of her own. Now that the Amoeba Boys were so smart, they could be used to solve the whole opposite problem!

"Oh, no!" Bubbles cried, popping out of her hiding place. "Thanks to the Professor's opposite potion being spread all over Townsville, you guys are now brilliant. Just promise me one thing—you won't invent any more opposite potion. If we Powerpuff Girls get oppositized, we'll be completely helpless."

"Really?" Bossman looked interested. "In that case...."

The Amoeba Boys raced out of the ice-cream parlor into the drugstore next door. Bubbles and her sisters followed and found them mixing up a bunch of ordinary household ingredients in a big glass jar. Bubbles winked at Blossom and Buttercup. The Amoeba Boys might be master criminals now, but they didn't know one very important thing—the Girls had *already* been affected by the opposite potion; however, the Girls *still* had all their superpowers.

"Aha!" Bossman cried, holding up the jar. It contained a bubbling purple potion. "Now you shall bow before us!"

Bubbles grabbed the potion out of Bossman's hands and quickly sprinkled the Amoeba Boys with it. They immediately returned to their usual non-clever selves.

"Thanks for the antidote, Boys," she said. "I thought a bunch of brilliant minds like yours would figure out that the opposite of opposite is the same. All we have to do is release the potion you made, and Townsville will return to normal."

The Amoeba Boys wailed, but it was too late. Bubbles had tricked them!

Continue on page 64.

Bubbles decided she and her sisters should search for the Professor at El Burrito Loco, one of his favorite places to eat. But when the Girls arrived, there was no sign of him.

"Now what?" Buttercup asked helplessly.

"I don't know," Bubbles admitted. Being a leader was hard!

The Girls slumped into a booth. Bubbles tried to figure out where to look next.

Suddenly, she noticed a baby sitting in a carriage at the next table while his mother ate lunch. That looked normal. But what *wasn't* so normal was that the baby was scribbling scientific formulas on a napkin!

Bubbles grabbed the napkin. "Excuse me," she told the baby's mother. "I just need to borrow this for a second."

She rushed to the café's kitchen. Her sisters followed.

"Pardon us," she said to the chef, who was busy taking a salad apart and flinging it around the room.

"What are you doing, Bubbles?" Blossom asked.

"According to the formula on this napkin, it looks like all we need are a few common ingredients to

make the antidote to the opposite potion!" Bubbles started grabbing things off the shelves: purple onions, black olives, baking soda, orange juice, and so on. Soon, she was holding a bubbling jar of purple liquid.

"What's that?" Buttercup asked.

"It's the antidote," Bubbles answered, heading for the kitchen door. "At least I *think* that's what it is...."

Bubbles rushed over to Ms. Keane. "We've got to stop this!" she exclaimed.

Ms. Keane looked up from the comic book she was reading. "Who says?"

"*I* say!" Bubbles replied. "Somebody might get hurt if we don't act fast!"

Bubbles's beloved teacher, usually so kind and responsible, just took a big bite of the candy bar she was holding. "I don't have to do nuthin'," she mumbled with her mouth full.

"Oh, no!" Bubbles cried. "You're oppositized, too!" Obviously, her teacher wasn't going to be any help at all.

Bubbles grabbed Ms. Keane's whistle and blew it. "Listen up, everybody!" she shouted to all of the kids. "I want you all to line up over here by the side of the road!"

Nobody even bothered to answer—except her kindergarten friend Mary. She turned around just long enough to stick out her tongue at Bubbles.

"Aargh!" Bubbles exclaimed to herself. "The whole Pokey Oaks class has turned into a bunch of troublemakers! Now what am I supposed to do?"

If Bubbles starts grabbing kids as she thought about doing before, turn to page 26.

If Bubbles blocks the road and then continues home to find the Professor, turn to page 24.

"Sorry, Princess," Bubbles said reluctantly. "We're busy right now."

"That's okay," Princess said. "I understand."

Just then, some people wandered past.

"Hold on!" Princess called, running toward the passersby. "Are you hungry? Can I buy you an ice-cream cone? Maybe a steak dinner? Or a pearl necklace?"

"I guess we'd better keep moving," Bubbles told her sisters. "We can keep an eye on Townsville while the Gangreen Gang is fetching the Professor."

They flew over the park. Blossom pointed down and giggled.

"Look!" she said. "It's those funny green boys again!"

"It's the Gangreen Gang!" Bubbles cried.

She flew down. The green-skinned gang was lined up along the street just outside the park.

"What are you doing?" Bubbles demanded. "You're supposed to be getting the Professor!"

"Sorry, Bubbles," Ace said with a shrug. "We had to stop and help these ants cross the street. Otherwise they could have been crushed!" He pointed to a line of tiny insects.

"Aargh!" Bubbles cried. "I guess we'll have to go find the Professor ourselves!"

Leaving the Gangreen Gang staring at the ants, Bubbles flew into the sky and rejoined her sisters.

Continue on page 22.

Bubbles decided to look for her sisters first. Then they could all spread out and search for the Professor.

Bubbles flew over Townsville and soon spotted Blossom and Buttercup in the park. They were playing jump rope with the Gangreen Gang.

"What's going on here?" Bubbles exclaimed as she flew down to them. Usually the sneaky, sly members of the Gangreen Gang spent all of their time causing trouble, not playing children's games.

Blossom giggled. "These nice green boys are lots of fun. I think we used to fight them."

"Whatever!" Bubbles dragged her sisters away from the game. "I just checked at home, and the Professor isn't there. We've got to search for him."

Buttercup's lower lip trembled. "Waaaa!" she cried. "We can't do this all by ourselves—we're just little girls! We have to find someone to help us!"

It just wasn't like Buttercup, her tough sister, to be so upset. Bubbles needed to find that antidote, and get things back to where they should be. Should she insist that they search for the Professor in some of his favorite spots? Or would Buttercup refuse to go along with the plan until they found someone else to help?

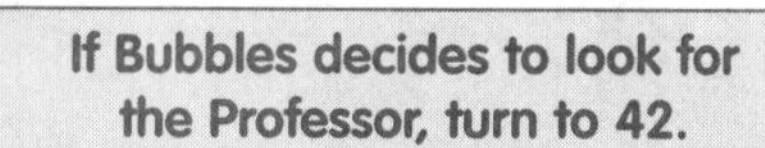

If Bubbles decides to look for the Professor, turn to 42.

If Bubbles decides to start asking some other grown-ups for help, turn to page 36.

"Should we try to stop the Amoeba Boys?" Buttercup asked nervously.

Bubbles shook her head. "The best way to stop them is to return them to normal right away, before they can plan another robbery," she said. "Once they're back to their usual selves, they'll be harmless again. We need to find that antidote!"

"But how?" Blossom asked. "We don't know where it is."

"We could hide out—er, I mean, *look* in the library," Buttercup suggested. "Or wait for some other superheroes to come along and help. . . ."

Continue on page 22.

Since the Girls were already at the bank, Bubbles decided to deal with the robbers before worrying about the opposite potion.

"Come on, Girls!" she cried. "Let's get those bad guys!"

Her sisters didn't move for a moment. Then Blossom flew straight up in the air, almost crashing into the ceiling. Meanwhile, Buttercup stared at the robbers fearfully.

Whew! Bubbles thought. *I guess my sisters can't help me. I'll have to handle these robbers on my own.*

She raced toward the closest criminal. He was busy handing out hundred-dollar bills to everyone in the bank.

"Why are you giving that money away?" Bubbles asked suspiciously. "You just stole it!"

"Yes, and we feel just awful about that," one of the robbers said with an embarrassed smile. "I don't know what we were thinking. I suppose the best thing to do is take ourselves off to jail so we can think about what we've done."

Bubbles blinked in surprise. "Actually, that's exactly what I was going to suggest," she said. "We'll take you to jail right now!"

"Oh, don't go out of your way, Girls," another robber said kindly. "We know the way. We'll be sure to lock ourselves up good and tight."

Just then, Bubbles glanced through the bank's windows. She saw a cat chasing a dog across the street and an elderly man turning cartwheels down the sidewalk.

Uh-oh. Things were really getting confusing out there—all thanks to the opposite potion. What should Bubbles and her sisters do now?

If Bubbles decides she and her sisters should escort the robbers to jail (just in case), turn to page 18.

If Bubbles decides to check out what trouble the opposite potion's causing in Townsville instead, turn to page 20.

Bubbles decided to check the Townsville Science Expo Center first.

The Professor was standing outside the center with Blossom and Buttercup!

Thank goodness! thought Bubbles in relief.

Bubbles flew down to them. "Hi, Professor," she said breathlessly. "Did you figure out an antidote?"

"Anti-wha?" the Professor said stupidly.

Bubbles groaned. Oh, no—the Professor was oppositized, too!

"He keeps going from stupid to smart and then back to stupid again," Buttercup said. "It happens every time the wind blows his wet sleeve against his arm."

Bubbles noticed that the Professor was holding a glass jar of purple potion. There was a big, wet purple stain on his sleeve. "It looks like the same stuff we spilled," she said thoughtfully. Suddenly, Bubbles figured it out. "Aha! The opposite of opposite is the same. Every time the Professor's arm gets wet, he's affected by the potion. And every time someone gets exposed to the potion again, the potion's effects are reversed!"

"I don't get it," Blossom said, looking uncharacteristically confused.

"Never mind." Bubbles grabbed the potion from the Professor. "All we need to do is release this all over Townsville, and everything should go back to normal!" Bubbles made the Professor take off his jacket and then sprinkled him with the potion. Then, she sprinkled herself and her sisters with the potion, too. Soon, the Professor and the Girls were all back to normal. Now, it was Townsville's turn to become de-oppositized!

Continue on page 64.

Bubbles decided she didn't have any time to waste finding her sisters. She had to find an antidote as soon as possible.

She raced toward home, taking a shortcut over Townsville Highway 1. As she flew over the busy road, she glanced down—and screeched to a stop. Her whole Pokey Oaks kindergarten class was playing right in the middle of the highway!

"Hey!" Bubbles cried, flying down toward them. "Get out of the road, you guys!"

Elmer Sglue looked up at her. "Betcha can't make me!" he taunted.

"Yeah!" cried twin brothers Floyd and Lloyd Floijoidson. "We can do whatever we want."

Bubbles groaned. The opposite potion was making all the nice kids in her class act like jerks! The only one who was behaving himself was Mitch Mitchelson, the class troublemaker. He was sitting quietly on the grass practicing his penmanship.

I've got to do something before they all get run over! Bubbles thought anxiously.

She was about to start grabbing kids and dragging them out of the road when she suddenly spotted their teacher, Ms. Keane, sitting by the side of the road. Maybe Ms. Keane could help her get the kids off the highway!

If Bubbles starts grabbing kids and carrying them to safety, turn to page 26.

If Bubbles asks Ms. Keane to help her get the kids off the highway, turn to page 44.

"You're right to wonder about Princess, Buttercup," Bubbles said. "She is *always* a suspicious character."

The Girls hurried over to see what Princess was doing. There was a huge pile of toys and clothes on the sidewalk beside her. She saw The Powerpuff Girls coming and waved.

"Hello, you three," she called. "How are you today?"

Bubbles blinked in surprise. It wasn't like Princess to worry about how anyone else was doing. Then again, nobody was acting like themselves that day. Why should Princess be any different?

"We're fine," Buttercup answered. "What are you doing?"

"I'm trying to give away all of my money and toys and clothes and things," said Princess, smiling.

Just then, a grouchy-looking man walked past. Princess handed him a huge gem.

"Gosh, thanks, little girl," the man exclaimed happily. "I've always wanted one of these!"

"Why are you giving your stuff away?" Bubbles asked Princess as the man skipped off.

Princess sighed. "That's the only way I can make my dreams come true and become a hermit."

"A her-what?" Blossom looked confused.

"A hermit," Bubbles explained. "That's someone who lives all by herself in a cave because she wants to lead a simple life."

"Right," Princess said eagerly. "Doesn't that sound wonderful?"

"Sure. That sounds just lovely—for you," Bubbles said.

"But first, I have to get rid of all my worldly things," Princess explained. "I even gave away the rare black pearl Daddy bought me last week!"

"That's nice," Bubbles said politely. Obviously, Princess wasn't going to cause them any trouble today!

Continue on page 13.

"Let's take a look around Townsville," Bubbles decided. "There's got to be another black pearl somewhere in the city."

The Girls started checking jewelry stores. At the last store they checked, they spotted a beautiful black pearl in the window.

"Aha!" Bubbles cried.

She flew toward the door, but before she reached it, a tall, thin man rushed out and shook his fist at them.

"Stop right there!" he cried. "Take your money and your credit cards and stay away from my store! I'm not letting anybody buy *any* of my jewelry!"

"Oh, no," Buttercup whispered. "He's been oppositized, and now he doesn't want to sell

anything! He's not going to let us buy the pearl!" She started to cry.

Bubbles saw that her sister was right. They could try to persuade the store owner to give them the pearl, but it would probably be very difficult. Maybe it would be better to go ask Princess to help the Girls find her pearl after all, even if it meant bringing Princess back to Townsville....

If the Girls decide to try to talk the jewelry store owner into giving them the pearl, turn to page 59.

If the Girls decide to bring Princess back and ask for her help, turn to page 8.

Bubbles couldn't resist giving Princess exactly what she wanted. This was their chance to rid Townsville of its most spoiled and annoying citizen!

"Come on, Princess," Bubbles said gleefully. "The mountaintop express leaves right now!"

The Girls took hold of Princess and flew her to the highest peak of Townsville Mountain. It was windy and bare there, with only a few scrawny trees growing outside of a tiny, rocky cave.

"It's wonderful!" Princess cried joyfully. "I must be the luckiest girl in the world!"

"Okay. If you say so," Bubbles said with a grin.

Boy, is Princess going to be surprised when she gets de-oppositized! Bubbles thought.

The Powerpuff Girls sped back down the mountain. As they flew over Townsville, Bubbles spied the Professor racing through the streets.

Continue on page 60.

"We don't have time to go get Princess," Bubbles decided. "We've got to have that pearl now! It's an emergency! Come on, Girls!"

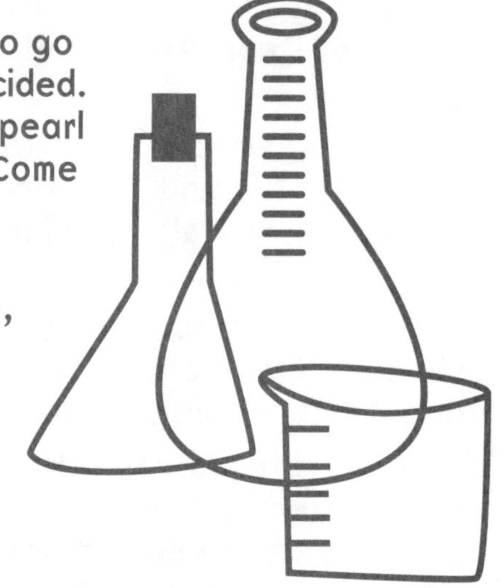

The Powerpuff Girls entered the jewelry store, but the store owner refused to give up the pearl. Then Bubbles had an idea. She held up the diamond bracelets that Princess had given them.

"Wouldn't you like to have these?" Bubbles said to the store owner.

"Oh, yes," he said greedily, snatching at the bracelets.

"Well, if you give us the pearl, we'll give you the bracelets."

"All right," the store owner said grudgingly. Soon, Bubbles had the pearl, and she and her sisters raced back home to the Professor, who was waiting for them.

"Did you get it?" he cried.

"Of course!" Bubbles said.

She handed over the pearl, and the Professor mixed it into the formula.

"There," he said, holding out the glass container. "This should do it!"

Continue on page 64.

"Professor! Professor!" The Girls flew down to greet him.

"Hello, Girls." The Professor looked worried. "I'm glad I found you. I have the antidote almost finished." He held up a jar of bubbling purple liquid.

Bubbles suddenly wondered if the Professor had been oppositized. "Are you sure you got it right?" she said. "I mean, I know you're usually smart about these things, but...."

The Professor chuckled. "Don't worry. I was oppositized for a while, but then I stumbled into a puddle of the spilled potion and went back to normal. That's how it works, you see—the opposite of opposite is the same. So, all I have to do is make more formula, and Townsville will be saved."

"Yay!" Bubbles cheered.

"There's a problem, though," the Professor said. "I'm missing one very important ingredient —a black pearl."

"I thought your formula was made out of ordinary household ingredients," Buttercup said.

The Professor shrugged sheepishly. "Black pearls are ordinary in *some* households—at least, in the households on pearl-diving islands," he said. "Unfortunately, Townsville *isn't* a pearl-diving island, so they're very, very rare here. I used the only pearl I had to make the first batch of the potion."

Bubbles remembered Princess's comment about the black pearl she'd given away. Maybe Princess could help them retrieve it. Or maybe it would be easier to look for another pearl on their own.

If Bubbles and her sisters bring Princess back to Townsville, turn to page 8.

If Bubbles and her sisters search for another black pearl instead, turn to page 56.

Better safe than sorry, Bubbles decided. With Townsville topsy-turvy, the last thing they needed was Mojo Jojo causing more trouble.

"Come on, Mojo," Bubbles said. "We'd better take you to jail just in case you change your mind and decide to commit a crime or something."

"Yes, of course," Mojo babbled. "Anything you wish of me is yours. I live only to serve the wonderful Powerpuff Girls. My life is in your dainty yet powerful hands."

Bubbles sighed. Mojo might be acting the opposite of his usual evil self in some ways, but he still talked a lot!

The Powerpuff Girls grabbed Mojo and flew toward the jail. The whole way there, Mojo kept telling The Powerpuff Girls how wonderful they were.

Bubbles wasn't really listening. She was too busy watching all the crazy things going on down below in the streets of Townsville.

Bubbles saw a street sweeper dumping garbage *out* of trash cans. She saw a dog walking a man on a leash. She even saw a kid toss aside an ice-cream cone and eagerly start munching a carrot stick instead!

By the time Bubbles dumped Mojo into his usual jail cell, she was very worried.

"We need to find the Professor and figure out how to fix this opposite potion mess," she told her sisters. "But things are already so crazy. Maybe we

should stop by the Mayor's office first to make sure there are no emergencies. What do you think?"

Buttercup shrugged. Blossom looked confused.

It was up to Bubbles to decide.

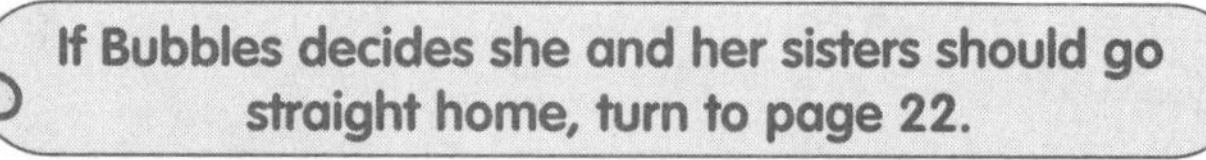

If Bubbles decides she and her sisters should go straight home, turn to page 22.

If Bubbles decides they should check in with the Mayor first, turn to page 10.

Holding the potion, the Girls flew high up into the sky. They spread the purple stuff all over Townsville.

Bubbles knew that if the potion worked, all the good changes—like criminals becoming good guys—would go away, along with the bad ones. But she didn't mind. She liked Townsville the way it usually was—villains and all.

"Did it work?" Buttercup wondered out loud.

They looked down.

"Look, the Gangreen Gang is picking on some little kids," Blossom cried. "We should come up with a plan to teach those rowdy ragamuffins a lesson!"

"Yeah!" Buttercup cried. "Let's go down there and pound them!"

"There's the Mayor," Bubbles exclaimed. "He just tied his shoes together and tripped over that cute little puppy!"

The Powerpuff Girls looked at one another and smiled. Townsville was back to normal—and so were they!

And so, once again, the day is saved, no thanks to—no, actually, thanks to—The Powerpuff Girls, and a certain purple potion!

THE END